This Book Belongs To:

....

....

Thanks again to the wonderful people at Tower Bridge for their ongoing support and inspiration.

Follow Bella the Tower Bridge Cat and her adventures at
TowerBridgeCat.com

Text copyright © Tee Dobinson 2022
Illustrations © Steve Cox 2022
Art direction and design – Ben Morris

Thanks to Jim Morris, Sara Fox and Steph Norris

The Tower Bridge Cat series is published by Baizdon Ltd
20 Coxton Street, Spondon, Derby, DE21 7JG
Baizdon.com

1 2 3 4 5 6 7 8 9 10 Published 2022. Printed in England

A CIP catalogue record for this book is available from the British Library

ISBN 978-1-7399937-0-2

The Tower Bridge CAT & the Missing Button

Written by **Tee Dobinson** and illustrated by **Steve Cox**

The Lord Mayor's Show is starting at Tower Bridge today.
Everywhere was sparkling with new paint and
Bella the Tower Bridge Cat
was looking forward to being in the grand parade.

Bella spotted that the Bridge hadn't closed. That's odd, she thought, the Lord Mayor's gold coach and all the fantastic floats won't be able to cross unless the Bridge is down.

Bella ran swiftly down to the Control Cabin to find out what was wrong.

Inside, the Bridge Master was looking horrified. "Bella, the Bridge is stuck open!" he cried. "The shiny silver button to close the Bridge has **vanished!**"

"It was here this morning for a Bridge Lift," said the puzzled Bridge Master. "I don't understand, buttons can't just go missing."

But as he turned to leave...

Miaow!

...his trousers **fell down!** The button holding them up had disappeared too!

"Bella, please find out what is happening!" implored the Bridge Master.

Bella found the twins in the Engine Rooms, looking confused.

"We can't finish our race, the start buttons have vanished!" exclaimed Eddie the Engineer. "It's spoiled our fun."

"Especially as I was winning!" added Olly the Oiler.

The Tower Bridge Cat continued her hurried investigations.

Hannah the Cook was looking very worried. "There is a mystery here in the kitchen Bella, there are no buttons left on my gingerbread team!"

"I won't be able to give them to the Lord Mayor now," sighed Hannah.

Miaow Miaow.
We've definitely got a problem now!

Everywhere Bella went she saw people with their buttons missing.

The Pearly King and Queen were mystified,
where had their lovely buttons gone?

Poppy the Painter was packing up her paint brushes when Bella asked her about the vanishing buttons. "There are buttons all over the Bridge," fumed Poppy.

Miaow?

"One even fell into my paint pot this morning.
And now I am stuck in my cradle as the down button is missing!"

It was tricky for people to get to the highest points on the Bridge, but not for the Tower Bridge Cat!

She crawled out of a window, tiptoed along a high ledge,

pushed open a dusty trap door, dashed speedily along a secret passage,

sprinted up some spiral stairs,

climbed up a wobbly ladder...

...raced along the **riveted rafters**...

...and squeezed through a little door to step outside onto a tiny roof ledge. Bella spotted one of the gold crests, she was at the **very top** of the South Tower!

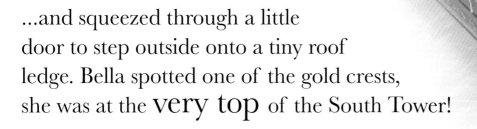

Miaow Miaow.
I have to be careful now!

Bella could see Poppy the Painter in her cradle and below her the gold coach and the parade. The Lord Mayor's Show was due to start in five minutes, but the Bridge was **still up!**

Bella was amazed to see a huge heap of brightly coloured buttons dazzling in the sunlight. On the top was the shiny silver button that closed the Bridge!

Bella clambered up towards the pile of glittering buttons.

Miaow Miaow!
I need that button now!

As Bella reached out and took the shiny silver button, a magpie
appeared and flew at her! He didn't want anyone to take
the treasures he had been collecting.

As Bella swerved away from him, the magpie
flapped his wings and accidentally
tipped Bella off the ledge!

Bella was falling...

...and falling...

...and falling!

Just in time the **quick-thinking** Tower Bridge Cat
called out to Poppy the Painter.

Poppy the Painter stretched her arms out...

...and caught Bella.

Phew!

Poppy the Painter quickly lowered them
down to the Control Cabin.
Would they get there in time for the
Lord Mayor's Show to start?

They made it!

Bella popped the shiny silver button into place and the Bridge Master,
wearing his spare trousers, firmly pressed it down.

The Bridge
started to close,
hooray!

The Tower Bridge Team were ready for the parade.

Eddie the Engineer helped Poppy the Painter climb on board the Tower Bridge float as Bella rushed past. She had to meet a special friend.

There was a big surprise for everyone as the Lord Mayor's gold coach led the parade across the Bridge – it wasn't just the Lord Mayor in the coach, the Tower Bridge Cat was in there too!

The Lord Mayor's Show paused in the City of London for speeches from the Lord Mayor and smiles from the Tower Bridge Cat. Then Poppy the Painter, the Bridge Master, Stan the Stoker, Eddie the Engineer, Olly the Oiler and Hannah the Cook waved to the crowds as everyone danced to the music of a jolly brass band.

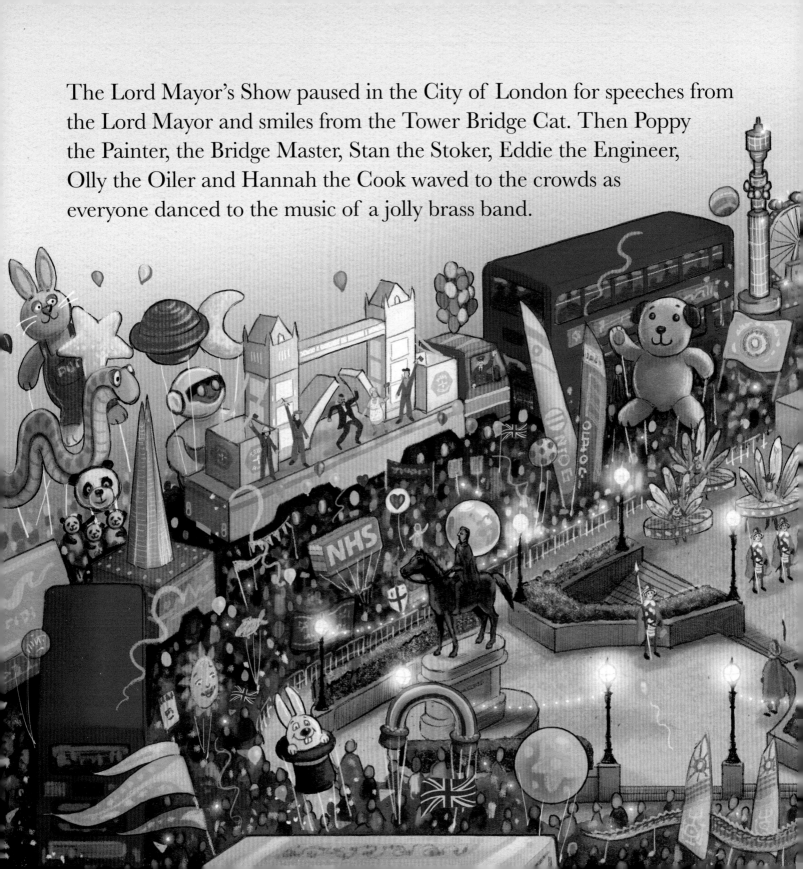

At the end of another exciting day, Bella and the magpie,
who had been busy giving back buttons all afternoon,
sat together and watched the sun go down over London.

*Miaow Miaow.
Everything is
purrrfect now!*

THE END

In Memory of Johnny Morris
1959-2020